Scratch, scratch, scratch.

"What's that?" Jake asked, her eyes wide.

"Don't be afraid," I said. "It's only Teddy playing a trick. He wants us to think there's a bear."

"But there *is* a bear," Jake said. "I heard Dad and the ranger talking about it. That's why Dad locked all the food in the car before we went to bed."

"There is a bear?" I felt chills run down my back.

Jake nodded. "He wandered down from somewhere and stays because of the food. The rangers want to catch him and take him back where he belongs."

Scratch, scratch, scratch.

I looked at the side of the tent where the noise came from. "But that can't be a bear. That's Teddy teasing us."

"But Teddy's asleep right over there," said Jake. And there he was, looking as sweet as I'd ever seen him.

"He sure looks nicer asleep than he does awake, doesn't he?" I said.

"Yes, he does," said Jake. "But, Scooter, if Teddy's asleep, then what's making that noise?"

Gayle Roper

CHARIOT
FAMILY
PUBLISHING
A DIVISION OF COOK COMMUNICATIONS

Chariot Family Publishing
Cook Communications, Colorado Springs, CO 80918
Cook Communications, Paris, Ontario
Kingsway Communications, Eastbourne, England

BEAR SCARE
© 1996 by Gayle Roper for text and Stephen J. Hunt for illustrations

Cover design by Joe Ragont
Cover illustration by J. Steven Hunt
First printing, 1996
Printed in The United States of America
00 99 98   5 4 3 2

Table of Contents

CHAPTER 1

"Teddy's going camping with us," said Dad.

"Teddy?" I said. "Oh, no!"

"With us?" said my sister, Jake.

"Teddy," said Dad. "With us."

"But Dad," I said, "he picks on Jake and me all the time."

Jake nodded. "And he likes to order us around."

"Please don't bring him, Dad," I said.

"Please?" said Jake.

Dad smiled. "Sorry, kids. It's all set. Teddy's looking forward to spending the weekend with you two. He told me so. You're his favorite cousins."

Dad walked out of the living room.

I looked at Jake. Her real name is Jacqueline Anne. I tell her she goes by Jake because she can't learn to spell Jacqueline. She's eight and in third grade. Most of the time Jake's a great sister. Most of the time.

I'm Scooter Grady. I'm seven and in second grade. I, of course, am always a great brother.

Our cousin Teddy is eleven and in fifth grade. He is not a nice kid, at least not to Jake and me. If he can make us mad or make us cry, he loves it.

"This is our first camping trip ever," said Jake. "I don't want it ruined by Teddy."

Later Jake came into my room while I was packing. She sighed. "Maybe he'll be afraid of the dark and go home early."

I pushed my pajamas and jeans and socks into my backpack. "I doubt it."

"You're right," Jake said. "He'll never be scared. He'll never go home. He'll just hang around us and make us unhappy."

"Who, me?" said a loud voice behind us. "Make you unhappy?"

We spun around to see Teddy standing in the doorway. He was grinning his nasty grin.

"Why, you're my favorite cousins," he said. He whacked me on the shoulder so hard that I almost fell over. I blinked back the tears and made believe it didn't hurt. Jake moved behind the bed where Teddy couldn't reach her.

He looked over his shoulder to see if Mom or Dad was near. I'd seen him check for adults before, and I knew what it meant—we were in trouble.

Teddy reached down and grabbed my backpack. He turned it over and dumped it all over the floor. Then he kicked my clothes under the bed. He put the backpack on my top closet shelf where I couldn't reach it.

Then he grinned his nasty grin at me. "You'd better get packed, Scooter," he said. "It's time to leave, and you're holding everyone up. Isn't he, Jake?"

CHAPTER 2

It seemed as if we drove forever before we reached our campground. The last little bit of the road went right across the top of the dam that made Bass Lake. We checked in at the rangers' station and drove to campsite #9, right on the lake's shore.

"Wow," I said as I ran down to the water's edge. "Let's go fishing, Dad. Maybe we can catch our dinner."

"No," said Jake. "Let's go swimming."

Mom and Dad stood by the car. They smiled at us and said, "Sorry, guys. First we set up camp. If you help, we'll be ready in no time."

"I'll go see where the rest rooms are," said Teddy.

"That's a good idea, Teddy," said Mom.

He walked off to search.

Jake and I ran around doing everything Dad asked us to do. We carried the tent and the tent pegs. We held ropes and handed Dad his tools when he wanted them. We helped put the tarp over the picnic table so we could eat even if it rained. We carried the Coleman stove to the table and helped Dad get water at the spigot down the road. We put the sleeping bags and backpacks in the tent. We stacked the wood for a campfire.

While we worked, Mom set up the kitchen and made dinner.

"Time to eat," she said as we stacked the last of the firewood.

I went right to the table. I was very hungry after all our hard work.

"Where's Teddy?" Dad asked as we sat down.

"Here I am, Uncle Marlin." Teddy walked up to the table and sat down. "I found the rest rooms. They're just around the corner over there." He pointed across the road.

"Thanks for finding them," said Mom. "You're just in time for dinner."

"Great," said Teddy. "I wouldn't want to miss any of your meals, Aunt Betty. You're such a good cook."

"Let's say grace," said Dad, bowing his head.

Teddy bowed his head like a little angel.

I bowed mine too, but I prayed my own prayer. *Lord, Teddy didn't do any work! He found the bathrooms almost across the road, and it took him forever. He's a jerk, and he didn't do any work!*

CHAPTER 3

When it got dark, Dad built a huge campfire. We sat around it and toasted marshmallows. I loved to put my marshmallow too close to the heat. When it caught on fire, it was like a torch. It was all black after I blew it out. It tasted sort of funny, but it looked great while it flamed.

After three torches, Mom made me stop.

"It's too dangerous, Scooter," she said. "Just brown the marshmallows. Don't burn them."

"Aw, Mom," I said. "It's fun to set them on fire."

Mom looked at me, and I knew she was going to have the last word. "No torches. You may have more marshmallows if you promise not to burn them."

"I'm not burning my marshmallows," said Teddy. "It's too dangerous."

"Thanks for being so careful, Teddy," said Dad.

I thought I was going to throw up. Teddy was such a jerk!

Finally Dad said, "Okay, kids. Time for bed."

All three of us said, "No! Not yet! Please!"

"Oh, yes," said Mom. "It's way past your usual time. To bed with you."

"But not me," said Teddy. He smiled at Mom and Dad. "I'm old enough to stay up later. Right, Aunt Betty? Right, Uncle Marlin?"

"Sorry, Teddy," said Mom. "You're turning in now too."

"What a shame, Teddy," I said. I made my voice sound as sweet and gooey as a marshmallow. "You have to go to bed with us little kids."

Teddy sort of snarled.

"You kids walk to the rest rooms with Mom," said Dad. "I'll stay here and keep an eye on the fire."

Teddy and I finished in the men's room at the same time. We came outside and looked for Mom and Jake.

"Let's walk back without them," said Teddy.

We started down the road. I was surprised at how dark it was out in the woods. The only light came from people's fires or lanterns. I was glad I had my flashlight in my hand.

Suddenly I sensed that Teddy and I weren't alone.

"Do you hear anything, Teddy?" I asked.

"It's just the bear I heard the ranger talking about," said Teddy. He growled like a very sick bear. "He's coming to get you."

"Right," I said. I didn't believe Teddy about the bear.

"I'm serious," he said. "There's a black bear who comes into the campground looking for food."

Suddenly I heard a snort beside me. I jumped a mile, and so did Teddy. I swung around and aimed my flashlight at the noise. Teddy and I both froze. For once he was as scared as I was.

Walking down the road with us was the biggest skunk I'd ever seen.

CHAPTER 4

The skunk stopped when Teddy and I did. He looked over his shoulder at me. Then he turned and looked at Teddy. He snorted again and started walking.

I was afraid even to breathe.

Just then a loud voice yelled, "Hey, Mom! There they are."

It was Jake, and I could hear her running down the road toward Teddy and me. The beam from her flashlight jumped all over the trees as she ran.

The skunk heard her coming too. He stopped and looked at Teddy and me again.

Stop, Jake! You're scaring him! I thought. But I was afraid to call out. I knew that if we scared him at all, the skunk would spray us. I shut my eyes and waited.

Stop, Jake, before he sprays!

The skunk snorted again. I opened my eyes a crack to see what was going on. I watched the

skunk walk to the side of the road and into the woods. He disappeared just as Jake shined her flashlight in my face and then in Teddy's.

"What do you two mean, leaving us?" she asked. Then she noticed that we were acting sort of dazed. "What's wrong?" she asked.

"We were just walking with a skunk," I said.

"And you almost made him spray us!" shouted Teddy. "You dumb girl! And get that stupid flashlight out of my eyes!"

Jake stared at Teddy. I could tell he had hurt her feelings.

"Easy, Teddy," I said. "She didn't know there was a skunk. You should apologize for talking like that."

I might get mad at Jake myself sometimes, but nobody else was going to talk to my sister so rudely if I could help it!

"Hah! You can't make me apologize," Teddy said. He ran away, back to our campsite.

When Jake and Mom and I got back, Teddy was sitting in a chair and staring into the fire. He didn't look at us as we walked past him into the tent.

"I wish he wasn't here," said Jake as she climbed into her sleeping bag.

I nodded as I lay down. "He's not my favorite person."

I don't remember falling asleep, but the next thing I remember was waking up to a scratching sound on the outside of the tent. I sat up.

My first thought was, "Teddy! He's playing a trick!"

CHAPTER 5

I grabbed my flashlight and shined it at Jake.
She blinked in its beam and sat up. She rubbed her
eyes.

"What's wrong?" she said.

"Shh," I whispered. "Listen."

Scratch, scratch, scratch.

"What's that?" she asked, her eyes wide.

"Don't be afraid," I said. "It's only Teddy
playing a trick. He wants us to think there's a
bear."

"But there *is* a bear," Jake said. "I heard Dad and
the ranger talking about it. That's why Dad locked
all the food in the car before we went to bed."

"There is a bear?" I felt chills run down my
back.

Jake nodded. "He wandered down from
somewhere and stays because of the food. The
rangers want to catch him and take him back where
he belongs."

Scratch, scratch, scratch.

I looked at the side of the tent where the noise came from. "But that can't be a bear. That's Teddy teasing us." For once I wanted Teddy to be playing a trick on me.

"But Teddy's asleep right over there," said Jake.

I shined my flashlight where she pointed. There he was, looking as sweet as I'd ever seen him.

"He sure looks nicer asleep than he does awake, doesn't he?" I said.

"Yes, he does," said Jake. "But, Scooter." She grabbed my arm. "If Teddy's asleep, then what's making that noise?"

Scratch, scratch, scratch.

"Hey," grumbled Teddy. "Get that light out of my face." He sat up and glared at Jake and me.

"Keep your voice down," I said. "You'll wake Mom and Dad."

"I'm awake," said Dad. He sounded sleepy.

"Me, too," said Mom. She sat up. "What are you kids doing awake in the middle of the night?"

"Listen," I said. "There's something outside."

Scratch, scratch, scratch.

"It's the bear!" yelled Teddy as he jumped out of his sleeping bag. He ran and hid between Mom and Dad. "It's the bear!"

Mom patted Teddy kindly on the back. "I don't think it's the bear. Is it, dear?" She looked at Dad.

Scratch, scratch, scratch.

"It's trying to get me!" said Teddy.

"Calm down, Teddy," said Dad. "I don't think anything wants to get you."

Mom patted him on the back some more.

Dad climbed out of his sleeping bag and went to the tent door. He unzipped it and peered outside. I climbed out of my sleeping bag and stood near him. It was scary not knowing what was out there. I wanted to be near Dad if he needed me—or I needed him.

Scratch, scratch, scratch.

Dad grabbed his flashlight and went out into the dark.

CHAPTER 6

"Be careful, Marlin," Mom said.

But Dad had gone around the corner of the tent, and we couldn't see him anymore. I held my breath, waiting to hear a growl and a scream.

Instead I heard Dad laugh and laugh.

We all crowded out of the tent and around the corner. When we saw what was in the beam of Dad's flashlight, we laughed as hard as he did.

There, jumping against our tent, was a fat toad. Every time he hit the tent, he slid down the side, making a scratching noise.

"What's he doing?" asked Jake.

Dad shook his head. "I don't know," he said. "Maybe he has a path he usually follows, and our tent is in his way."

I reached down and picked up the fat guy. I carried him to the other side of our campsite, away from the tent. Then I put him down, and we all watched him jump away.

"Boy, he sure scared me," said Jake.

"Me, too," I said.

"Me, too," said Mom.

"He didn't do my heart any good either," said Dad.

"Well, I wasn't afraid," said Teddy. "I wasn't afraid at all." And he went into the tent.

I looked at Jake, and she looked at me.

"He was so scared," said Jake.

"Way scared," I said. "He hid between Mom and Dad."

Jake shivered. "I'm cold. Let's get back to bed."

When we woke up the next morning, the sun was shining brightly. I couldn't believe how scared we'd all been in the dark of night.

After breakfast Dad, Teddy, Jake, and I walked around Bass Lake to the boat rental area. The wind was blowing hard, but it was a warm wind, so it didn't bother us. Jake and I had fun throwing leaves up in the air and seeing where the wind took them.

"Dumb," said Teddy while Dad was talking to the boat man. "Throw something that makes sense. Like rocks." He threw a big rock and made a big splash.

"I can throw a lot better than you two can," he said. "Look how far my rock goes."

"Of course you can throw better than we can," I said. I watched his rock go far out into the lake. "You're lots older than we are."

"And don't you ever forget it," Teddy said. He stared at me with his extra-mean look.

Dad called us over to a rowboat, and Teddy, Jake, and I hurried to climb in.

"Just a minute, you guys," Dad said. "I have two very important rules you need to know about. You are never to get in the boat without me. And you must always wear your life jackets. Do you understand?"

I nodded and Jake nodded.

"Teddy, do you understand?"

"Sure, Uncle Marlin," he said. "I understand."

"Okay," said Dad. "I'm counting on all of you."

We set off across the lake, rowing back to our campsite.

It was very windy out on the water. Dad had to pull hard on the oars to make us go anywhere. Sometimes it seemed that every stroke Dad took, the wind undid.

"We'll never get back!" shouted Teddy. "We'll be on the lake forever."

I looked at Teddy and saw that he was scared.

Dad stopped rowing and turned to him. "Don't worry," he said. "We'll be fine."

While Dad was talking, the wind blew us farther across the water.

"Oh, no!" shouted Teddy. "We're going to go over the dam!"

CHAPTER
7

"Teddy!" said Dad. "The dam's at the end of the lake."

"I know. It's huge," he said. "We drove over it when we came. We're going to get sucked over it!"

"But we're not at the end of the lake," said Dad. "The dam is very far away. We're fine. There's a point of land between us and the dam. See? There's our campsite on this side of the point."

"But the wind's blowing us," Teddy said. "It'll blow us around the point!"

"No, it won't, Teddy," Dad said. "It's not blowing that hard. We're fine." He began to row again.

When we tied up at our campsite, Teddy jumped out of the boat as fast as he could. He pulled off his life jacket and threw it into the boat.

"I'm not going fishing," said Teddy. "It's too dangerous."

I looked at Teddy. I didn't understand him at all. On one hand, he was a bully who loved to pick on Jake and me. On the other hand, he was a big scaredy cat. How could he be both?

"We'll make an anchor to use while we fish," Dad said. "It'll keep us from being blown around."

"How can we make an anchor?" I asked.

"We'll fill a milk jug with little stones," said Dad. "That'll be your job, kids. We'll go fishing as soon as you're done."

I got an empty milk jug from the recycling bin by the rest rooms. Jake and I started putting stones from the edge of the road into it.

"You keep getting stones here, Jake," I said. "I'll get some by the edge of the lake."

Teddy came with me to the edge of the lake, but he didn't help.

"Are you afraid of getting your hands dirty?" I asked him.

Suddenly Teddy jumped.

"There's something in the bushes," he whispered.

I looked at the bushes right near us. Sure enough, they were shaking and moving. I could hear something snorting in them. Something big . . . and coming our way!

"Get in the boat!" yelled Teddy. "Quick! The bear won't get us in the boat!"

I jumped in, and he jumped in after me. We

"It's all your fault!" Teddy yelled at me.

I stopped trying to hook my life jacket and stared at him. "My fault?"

He nodded. His face was very pale. "If you hadn't moved around so much, the boat wouldn't have come loose."

"What?" I said. "*You're* the one who moved around."

"Hah!" he said.

"Think, Teddy," I said. "It wasn't me. You were the one who climbed to the backseat. You were the one who grabbed the oar. You were the one who almost tipped the boat."

He thought. "Oh," he said.

I waited for him to say he was sorry for blaming me. He didn't. What a jerk.

I went back to trying to hook my life jacket buckles. I finally got the last buckle to click. I felt much safer.

I looked up and saw we were still on the good side of the point.

"Can you swim?" I asked.

"A little bit."

"We'd better start rowing," I said.

Teddy didn't look as though he'd heard me. His eyes were too wide and too bright. He was shaking with fear.

I reached for an oar.

"I've got an idea," said Teddy. He licked his lips nervously. "I'm going to save us."

"How are you going to do that?"

"Look," he said. "We're not too far from land yet. I bet the water's not even deep. I'll just push us back."

"How can you push us out here in the lake?"

"Just watch," he said.

Before I knew what was happening, Teddy jumped out of the boat and right into the water. The only problem was that the lake was already deep. He went down and down under the water.

CHAPTER
9

"Teddy!" I watched my cousin sink down into the clear water. "Don't drown!"

Please, God! I prayed. *Don't let him drown! He might be a jerk, but I don't want him to drown!*

He didn't. He came right back up, like a bouncing ball. He was choking and spitting water, but he floated on the top in his life jacket.

I picked up an oar, surprised at how heavy it was.

"Here, Teddy!" I called. "Grab the oar!"

I held it on top of the water, and Teddy grabbed it. He pulled himself along the oar. Soon he grabbed hold of the boat. It rocked wildly, and I almost fell in with him.

"Be careful!" I yelled. "You'll tip the boat over."

Teddy didn't listen to me. He tried to climb in again.

"Wait, Teddy!" I cried. "Let me get in the back and sit down. Then you climb in near the front.

Maybe the boat won't tip so much that way."

I climbed to the back as fast as I could. I sat down and prayed, *God, help him get in the boat without tipping us over!*

"Okay," I called. "Now."

Teddy threw one leg over the side of the boat and sort of rolled in. The boat tilted, but not as far as before.

Teddy lay on the bottom of the boat in a big heap. I climbed over to him.

"Are you all right?" I asked.

He rolled over onto his back and swallowed a couple of times. "I'm fine," he said. "I wasn't scared."

"I sure was," I said. "I thought you were going to drown."

"When you're scared, you're a baby," said Teddy.

"When you're scared, then you pray," I said.

Teddy pulled himself up to the middle seat.

"Give me the oars, Scooter," he said. "I'll row us to shore."

I pushed one of the heavy oars to him and turned for the other.

"Where's the other one?" I said.

It wasn't in the boat. It was floating in the water too far away for us to reach.

CHAPTER 10

"Oh, no! We're going over the dam!" yelled Teddy again.

"Teddy," I said. "We're not even near the dam. Try to be brave for a change, okay? Just pray!"

I looked toward shore. It wasn't too far away. I just didn't know how to get us there. That's when I saw Jake.

She was running along the shore, looking at us. She was shouting something, but I couldn't hear her. The wind blew her words away.

Then she pointed. I looked where she pointed and saw a big pine tree lying on its side in the lake. It must have been very tall before it fell over. Now it lay there, reaching way out into the water.

"Look, Teddy!" I grabbed my cousin by the arm. "See that pine tree sticking out into the lake?"

Teddy looked. "So what?" he said.

"We just row toward that tree," I said. "Then we grab onto it before we get blown around the point."

"But we only have one oar," Teddy said.

I thought for a minute. "The wind is blowing us on one side," I said. "We'll row on the other."

And that's what we did. We sat on the middle seat and rowed together. It was hard for two reasons. One, the wind was strong, and two, Teddy's arms were longer than mine. But we pulled and pulled on the oar, and we got closer and closer to land.

Suddenly we were in the branches of the big pine tree. It was like being eaten by an animal with prickly teeth.

One branch scratched me on the arm, but I didn't care. I grabbed hold, and so did Teddy. He tried to climb out onto the tree. As soon as he put weight on the tree, it started to sink. He jumped back into the boat, and we almost tipped over. Again.

"Don't, Teddy!" I yelled. "You're making the boat tip and the tree shake."

"I'm not making the tree shake," Teddy said.

He wasn't. It was Jake, climbing out to us.

"Don't come any closer," I called. "The tree isn't safe."

"Then throw me your rope," she called back. "I'll tie you so you can't blow away!"

"We'll just tie up where we are," said Teddy.

He grabbed the rope and wrapped it around a

branch. The only problem was that we were near the tip of the tree. The branches were small, and they broke easily. The wind blew and the branch snapped, and we were loose again.

Teddy screamed and grabbed at the tree. He caught a handful of branches and held us. I climbed carefully to the front of the boat and threw the rope toward Jake. It didn't go far enough.

"Let me," said Teddy. "I can throw better than you can."

He climbed to the front of the boat and pulled the rope back in. Then he got ready to throw.

"Who's holding onto the tree?" I said.

Teddy and I both screamed and grabbed a branch. We were just in time. The wind already had blown us to the very tip of the tree.

I held on with both hands. The branches bent, and I knew they wouldn't hold us long.

Dear Lord, I prayed, *don't let the branches snap!*

"Hurry and throw the rope, Teddy," I said.

Teddy threw, and I watched the rope fly through the air.

Dear Lord, help the rope go far enough. Help Jake tie it tight, so we can pull ourselves in. Don't let us go around the point. Please!

The rope sailed through the air, right to Jake. She grabbed it and climbed back to shore with it.

She wrapped it around a strong tree two times.
Then she sat on the ground and held its end with
both hands.

"Okay!" she yelled. "Pull yourselves in."

Teddy and I pulled on the rope, and in no time
we were at the shore. With a great sigh we climbed
out of the boat and onto the ground.

My knees were so weak, I couldn't stand. I just
collapsed on the ground.

Thank You, God. Oh, thank You!

CHAPTER 11

Dad was real nice to Teddy and me. After he made Teddy change his wet clothes, he hardly yelled at all. He knew we hadn't tried to disobey. It just sort of happened.

"Besides, you were so scared by your adventure that you'll be careful it doesn't happen again," Dad said.

"I wasn't scared," Teddy said.

"Well, you should have been," said Dad.

"I was," I said. "I prayed."

"Me, too," said Jake.

Dad nodded. "That's good."

After lunch we fished for a while. We also went swimming. We cooked hamburgers and hot dogs over the campfire for supper. Then we went to a talk the ranger gave about the park.

"There's been a black bear roaming the campground," he said. "We want to catch him and take him back to the mountains. If you see him, let us know."

We walked back to our campsite after the ranger's talk. Just as we got to #9, there was a large crash by our picnic table.

"What was that?" I tried to see through the darkness.

"It's the bear!" said Teddy, jumping behind Dad.

Dad shined his flashlight toward the sound. Sitting on our picnic table and licking his paws was a fat, fat raccoon.

He blinked in the light, turned, and jumped off the table. He waddled into the bushes.

"Oh, wasn't he cute!" said Jake. "Did you see his mask?"

"I want to know what he was eating," said Mom. "I thought we put everything away before we went to hear the ranger."

We searched all around the table and found what the raccoon had been eating. It was Dad's favorite pecan pie. All that was left was the empty pie tin.

"I'm sorry," said Dad. "I got it out for an extra piece, and I forgot to put it away."

"I'm just glad it was a raccoon, not the bear," said Mom.

Dad built us another campfire, and we toasted marshmallows. I got to make two torches before Mom yelled at me again.

A loud snarl made me drop my third marshmallow in my lap.

"It's the bear!" screamed Teddy.

CHAPTER 12

We all jumped from our chairs and shined our flashlights at the horrible noise. I was sure we'd see the bear up on his hind feet, ready to attack. I was sure he'd look ten feet tall. I was sure he was going to eat us.

Instead we saw our raccoon fighting with a skunk over what looked like a hamburger.

"Hey, Teddy," I said. "It's your skunk."

Teddy came out from his hiding place behind Dad. "It's not my skunk," he said. "It's yours."

I grinned. "Let's say it's ours," I said. "We can share him."

My mom wasn't too happy. "It looks as though we're pretty careless campers," she said. "Dad's pecan pie wasn't the only food we overlooked."

The two animals snarled and growled. They wrapped their paws around each other and rolled over and over.

"Oh, no!" said Dad. "They've rolled under the car! What if the skunk decides to spray? Our car will smell bad forever."

We sat back down in our seats and listened to the animals. We couldn't tell which one was winning because we couldn't see under the car.

The skunk and the raccoon snarled and growled as long as it took me to toast another marshmallow. Then there was silence.

We all looked at the car to see who won the fight. Out walked the skunk. It went right to the hamburger and began eating. I heard a noise on the road and shined my flashlight. The raccoon was walking away.

"Poor raccoon," said Jake. "That was his dinner, not the skunk's."

"You want to tell the skunk?" I asked.

The next morning after breakfast we went to church right in the campground. We sat by the lake on seats made of logs. The leader played a guitar, and one man played bagpipes.

"That was so boring," said Teddy as we walked back to #9.

"I thought it was neat," I said.

"You wouldn't know neat if it bit you," Teddy said.

I looked at Teddy. I wanted to like him. He was my cousin. But he sure made it hard.

"Are you ever happy, Teddy?" asked Jake.

Teddy looked at her as though she were crazy. Then he walked away from us.

"I don't know if he's ever happy," I said. "But I do know he's afraid a lot."

"That's because he doesn't trust God to take care of him," Jake said.

When we got back to the campsite, Mom said, "We're going to eat our dinner now even if it's lunchtime. We'll be driving home at dinnertime."

We cooked steaks over the fire. Mom made a big salad and some peas, which I could have done without. We all took our seats, and Dad said grace. Before he said amen, I opened my eyes . . . and looked right into the eyes of the bear.

43

CHAPTER 13

"Dad," I said. My voice came out funny because I was so scared. "The bear's watching us." I stood up, ready to run.

"Right, Scooter," said Dad. His back was to the bear. So was Mom's.

Jake looked up. "Scooter's not kidding, Dad," she said as she climbed out of the picnic bench. "The bear really is watching us!"

Dad and Mom turned and gasped.

The bear started toward us.

"He wants to eat me!" screamed Teddy. "I knew he'd get me! I knew it!"

"Listen, everyone," said Dad. "Walk calmly to the car and get in. He's not interested in us. He wants our steaks."

"He wants me," cried Teddy, tears rolling down his cheeks.

Jake and I reached the car at the same moment. She opened the back door and fell in. I opened the front door and fell in. Mom jumped in after Jake, and Dad jumped in after me. We slammed the doors.

"Wait a minute," said Dad. "Where's Teddy?"

We all looked. Teddy was still at the picnic table, crying like crazy. The bear stood across from him, a steak in his paw.

Dad opened the door of the car. "Teddy!" he called. "Come here this instant!"

Dear Lord, I prayed. *Let Teddy be brave enough to get up and come to the car. And please keep him safe from the bear.*

"Let him eat me, Uncle Marlin," cried Teddy. "Then he won't eat you or Aunt Betty or Jake or Scooter."

"Teddy," said Dad as he climbed out of the car. "The bear doesn't want to eat you. He wants to eat our steaks. If you get up slowly and walk to the car, you'll be fine."

I looked at Teddy. He was scared. Boy, was he scared. But he was going to let the bear eat him to keep us safe. Now I really didn't understand him! I thought he hated us.

"Come on, Teddy," I called. "We'll go get the ranger to shoot the bear with a dart and put him to sleep. Then they can take him back to the mountains. He'll be fine. And so will you."

The bear grabbed another steak.

"Come on, Teddy," called Jake, "before the steaks are all gone. Then he might get mad."

"Come on, Teddy," said Mom. "You've been very brave. Now be smart, too."

Slowly Teddy got up. The bear didn't even look at him. Teddy stepped over the picnic bench. The bear grabbed another steak and a pawful of peas. Teddy ran for the car. The bear spit out the peas.

When Teddy jumped in the car, Jake and Mom hugged him and hugged him.

"You were wonderful, Teddy," said Mom.

I looked at Dad. "He was stupid," I said.

"Shush," said Dad. He started the car. "Let the girls think he was great. It'll help him feel better."

"What do you mean?" I asked. "Does he feel bad?"

Dad nodded. "He thinks no one likes him."

"He's right," I said.

Dad pulled into the ranger's station.

"He should pray about his problems," I said. "I prayed, and God helped me. Lots of times."

Dad smiled at me. "I think I'll pray that Teddy gets to be as smart as you, Scooter."

We got to follow the ranger back to our campsite and watch from our car while he shot the bear with a dart. The ranger and some other men put the bear in a cage. Then they put the cage on a truck and drove away.

"When he wakes up," said the ranger, "he'll be far, far away in the mountains. He'll eat natural food and be happier and healthier."

By the time all the action was over, it was time to take our tent down and go home.

"Can we come camping again?" I asked Dad.

"You want to?" he said. "You're not afraid to try again?"

"I was scared sometimes," I said. "But not too scared."

"The same for me," said Jake.

"I wasn't afraid," said Teddy. "Not at all."

We all stared at him.

"Well," he said. "Maybe just a little."

I smiled at Teddy. "It's okay to be scared," I said.

"Just as long as you remember to pray," said Jake.

My sister and I looked at each other, then I nodded. I turned to Teddy.

"Next time we come camping," I said, "we

want you to come too, Teddy."

"Do you really?" asked Teddy.

"Yes," said Jake. "We really do."